™

Special thanks to
Emily Sharratt

Reading Consultant: Prue Goodwin, lecturer in literacy and children's books.

ORCHARD BOOKS

First published in 2020 by The Watts Publishing Group

7 9 10 8 6

A CIP catalogue record for this book is available from the British Library.

ISBN 978 1 40835 470 4

Printed and bound in China

The paper and board used in this book are made from wood from responsible sources.

Orchard Books
An imprint of Hachette Children's Group
Part of The Watts Publishing Group Limited
Carmelite House, 50 Victoria Embankment, London EC4Y 0DZ

An Hachette UK Company
www.hachette.co.uk
www.hachettechildrens.co.uk

TEAM ROCKET
TROUBLE

ORCHARD

MEET ASH AND PIKACHU!

ASH
A Pokémon dreamer who wants to have it all – including becoming a Pokémon Master!

PIKACHU
Ash's first partner Pokémon and long-time companion!

LOOK OUT FOR THESE POKÉMON

BEWEAR

MEOWTH

GARDEVOIR

MIMIKYU

HAUNTER

CONTENTS

PART ONE: NEW ARRIVALS

PART TWO: THE DISGUISE POKÉMON

PART THREE: POKÉMON BATTLE

PART ONE
New Arrivals

CHAPTER ONE

Team Rocket

There were four new arrivals at the airport on Melemele Island in the Alola region: Jessie and James, and their Pokémon Meowth and Wobbuffet. They made up Team Rocket, and they were Ash's old enemies.

"At last, we're here," said Jessie, adjusting her sunglasses.

"And we're going to catch as many rare Pokémon as we can for our boss," said James.

"First we'll capture Pokémon …" began Jessie.

"And then we'll rule Alola," continued James, with a nasty smile.

Elsewhere on Alola, Ash received a strangely shaped Pokédex from Professor Kukui at the Pokémon School.

"It's time to activate your Pokédex," said the professor.

He tapped at the keyboard of his computer and then smiled. "There we go," he said, as the lights in the room began to spark and crackle. "You're all connected now."

"What do you mean? What's going on?" said Ash, looking at the flashing lights in alarm.

Suddenly, a tiny Pokémon burst out of one of the sockets in the wall.

"It's a Rotom!" shouted Ash.

The Rotom whizzed around the room, making Ash's head spin. Then, without warning, it flung itself at the Pokédex and disappeared inside.

As Ash looked at the Pokédex in astonishment, a face appeared in its centre and it began to move.

"Alola, nice to meet you, Ash," the Pokédex declared.

CHAPTER TWO

Meet Rotom Dex

"You can talk!" Ash said to the Pokédex in surprise.

"Of course," the Pokédex replied. "I am Rotom Dex and I have been programmed with many different languages to communicate with anybody!"

"Awesome!" Ash exclaimed.

"Awesome?" Rotom Dex responded. "Does not compute."

"Ash is saying that he is impressed by what you can do," Professor Kukui explained.

"I understand!" Rotom Dex

declared. "Awesome means excellent. So Rotom Dex is excellent!"

Ash introduced Rotom Dex to Pikachu and then to the professor's Pokémon, Rockruff. Rotom Dex took photographs.

It added the Pokémon to its database.

"Rotom Dex, can you tell me what you already know about Pikachu?" Ash asked.

"Of course, Ash!" Rotom Dex replied. "Pikachu, the Mouse Pokémon, is an Electric type.

It raises its tail to sense its surroundings. If you pull on its tail, it will bite."

Rotom Dex moved behind Pikachu and demonstrated by pulling hard on its tail.

Pikachu reacted by using the move Thunderbolt.

It gave them all a big electric shock.

"Oh!" said Rotom Dex. "It doesn't bite, it shocks!"

CHAPTER THREE

Pokémon Search

Later, in the Pokémon School, Ash was introducing his Alolan friends to Rotom Dex.

"Nice to meet you," it said.

"A Pokédex with a Rotom inside!" said Lillie. "Incredible!"

"Incredible," repeated Rotom Dex. "That means awesome!"

"Ah, so it has learned how Ash speaks," said Sophocles, reaching for his screwdriver. "Fascinating! I wonder how it is programmed."

Rotom Dex moved backwards nervously.

"Let me just have a quick look at how you work, OK?" said Sophocles.

"No, thank you!" Rotom Dex replied nervously, its voice quavering.

Luckily, at that moment, Professor Kukui arrived.

"All right, class," the professor called, "today you're going to do field work. With Ash's new Rotom Dex, you should be able to catch Pokémon."

The class cheered. "Let's go!"

Meanwhile, Team Rocket were
walking through the
Alola forests, searching for
Pokémon too.

"It's rather creepy out here,"
Jessie said, looking around
the shadowy trees. "It feels as
though something scary could
jump out at any moment."

Just then, they heard some
rustling nearby. A strange new
Pokémon burst out of the
bushes.

PART TWO
The Disguise Pokémon

CHAPTER FOUR

Mystery Pokémon

Jessie, James, Meowth and Wobbuffet all screamed. They clung to each other in fright.

The new Pokémon was very strange looking.

"Pikachu?" Jessie asked. The Pokémon didn't respond.

"No," said Meowth. "If you look closer you can see that it's some other Pokémon disguised as a Pikachu."

The mystery Pokémon juddered, making funny sounds.

Meowth and Wobbuffet were still keeping well back.

"What's wrong?" asked James. "What is it saying?"

"It's too scary to repeat," Meowth said, not taking its eyes off the Pokémon.

"Scary?" repeated Jessie. "Don't be silly. It's cute!"

"Let's make it the first
Pokémon we capture in the
Alola region!" Jessie seized
Meowth and flung him
forwards. "Meowth, use
Fury Swipes!"

As Meowth flew through the

air towards the Pokémon, it got ready to do battle. "OK, here we go!" it said reluctantly as it landed.

Meowth's long claws shone in the light as it took aim at the Pokémon.

But the other Pokémon barely seemed to notice, only turning to repeat the strange sounds once again.

"Stop with all that tough talk!" Meowth said, trembling. "Take off that Pikachu costume

and fight fairly!"

Suddenly feeling angry, Meowth leaped forwards, pulling at the edge of the Pikachu costume.

The next thing Meowth knew, everything had gone very dark!

CHAPTER FIVE

Meowth's Dream

When Meowth next opened
its eyes, it was in a long
dark tunnel.

"Where am I?" said Meowth,
feeling more scared than ever.
"Jessie? James? Wobbuffet?"

A light appeared at the end

of the tunnel. "A way out of here!" cried Meowth, running towards it.

The light became brighter until Meowth came to a field of colourful flowers. In his path floated beautiful Gardevoir, Glaceon and Lopunny.

They waved at Meowth,
seeming to call it on.

Meowth's eyes widened in
delight as it flung its arms
open. It followed after them,
skipping happily. But behind
Meowth followed scary Gastly,
Haunter and Gengar.

"Meowth! Meowth!" Jessie and James's voices – followed by the splash of cold water – brought Meowth back from its crazy dream.

"What's wrong with you?" Jessie asked impatiently.

"You weren't even attacked!"

"I'm so glad to be back!" Meowth cried, flinging its arms around Jessie and James.

"Back?" said James.

"Yes," Meowth replied. "As soon as I looked under

that weird Pokémon's costume, I went to a scary place. I don't know how I would have got back without you!"

Before Jessie or James could ask Meowth any more, there was a rustling of branches and the sound of approaching feet.

"Quick, hide!" shouted Jessie in fright.

CHAPTER SIX

Mimikyu

As Team Rocket looked on from their hiding place behind some trees, Ash and his friends were walking through the forest towards them.

"I've got a feeling we're going to find a wild Pokémon

very soon," said Ash happily.

"I hope so," replied Sophocles. "I'm getting tired from all this walking."

"Ash and Pikachu!" muttered James through clenched teeth.

Jessie leaned closer and hissed, "Yes, and with them are lots of Alola Pokémon! This is a great chance for us to capture Pikachu and many more! The boss will be so pleased with us!"

"Look!" they heard Ash shout. He had spotted the mystery Pokémon.

"Pika!" said Pikachu in delight.

"I don't think it's a Pikachu," said Lana.

"I've read about this Pokémon. It's a Mimikyu. I think it …" said Lillie.

"Leave the Pokémon descriptions to me!" interrupted Rotom Dex. "Mimikyu is the Disguise Pokémon. It is a Ghost and Fairy type. It wears a ragged head cover to look like a Pikachu. Little more is known about this Pokémon."

"Cool!" said Ash. "OK, Pikachu – go and get Mimikyu!"

"Pikachu!" replied his Pokémon in agreement, turning to face Mimikyu.

"Pikachu, use Iron Tail!" cried Ash.

Pikachu leaped into the air, its tail glowing brightly. It crashed down on top of Mimikyu.

The Disguise Pokémon appeared to crumple.

Then it rose up again, completely unharmed.

Mimikyu threw itself into a counter-attack, hitting at Pikachu with its own tail.

"This Pokémon is really strong!" shouted Ash.

PART THREE

Pokémon Battle

CHAPTER SEVEN

Old Enemies

Before Pikachu had a chance to recover from the last attack, Mimikyu zapped it with an electric charge.

"Close-range combat is too dangerous," Ash said worriedly. "Pikachu, use Electro Ball!"

Pikachu moved backwards, creating a crackling ball of energy with its tail. Once the ball was big enough, Pikachu fired this at Mimikyu. But Mimikyu simply batted it back with its tail. Pikachu had to duck out of the way to avoid being hit by its own Electro Ball attack!

"Are you OK?" Ash called to Pikachu.

"Pika, pika," Pikachu replied, nodding.

"Good," Ash said.

"It's your move, Pikachu!"

"Just a minute," said Jessie, stepping onto the path.

"Who are you?" asked Kiawe.

"Who are we?" replied James. He and Jessie both laughed.

"We're Team Rocket," they declared together.

"Team Rocket?" repeated Rotom Dex. "Does not compute."

"We're a super-powerful evil organisation," James said, with an impatient roll of his eyes.

"What sort of silly Pokédex doesn't know an important thing like that?" Meowth demanded.

"A Meowth that can speak like a human!" Rotom Dex spluttered.

"I do not have any data on this!"

"Well, I've never heard of Team Rocket either," declared Mallow.

"Nor me," agreed Lillie.

"They're bad guys who steal other people's Pokémon," said Ash, scowling. His Alolan friends drew nearer to their own Pokémon.

"Correct," said Jessie with a smirk. "And we're going to start with that Mimikyu."

CHAPTER EIGHT

Meowth vs Pikachu

"OK, Meowth," Jessie said. "Let's go!" Pikachu stepped into Meowth's path. "You'd better deal with Pikachu first."

"Ohhh," Meowth moaned, but one look at Jessie silenced its complaints.

"All right, Pikachu. Prepare for my Fury Swipes move!"

Once again, Meowth pounced, claws flashing.

"Pikachu," Ash called quickly, "use Electro Ball!"

Pikachu's ball of crackling energy hurtled towards Meowth. Just in time, Mimikyu threw a counter Shadow Ball attack. It knocked Electro Ball out of the way.

"Mimikyu!" Meowth exclaimed in surprise. "You saved me — thank you!"

Mimikyu turned towards Meowth, making its strange rumbling sounds again.

"Whoa!" Meowth exclaimed. "Mimikyu wants to help us!"

"Well, never mind why it's on our side," Jessie said. "Mimikyu, attack!"

Mimikyu began to create another ball of energy.

"Get ready, Pikachu!" called Ash.

But before anyone knew what was happening, a huge pink Pokémon crashed out of the bushes. It took Jessie and James, one under each of its massive arms.

Meowth and Wobbuffet could only look on in surprise as the giant Pokémon turned and walked away. It carried the rest of Team Rocket.

They called after it, but
it simply trudged onwards.
Jessie and James squirmed
and squealed in its arms.

CHAPTER NINE

Bewear

"Who is that Pokémon?" Ash asked, his mouth open. He thought it looked familiar.

"Bewear," replied Rotom Dex, "the Strong Arm Pokémon. It is a Normal and Fighting type. Bewear has very powerful arms and is extremely dangerous. It waves in what looks like a friendly manner, but this is in fact a warning signal. Approach with caution."

"Oh yeah," said Ash. He remembered how he and Pikachu had seen Bewear when they had first arrived in the Alola region. They had ended up having to run away from it.

Mimikyu was still facing Pikachu, its ball of dark energy hovering above.

"Mimikyu!" bellowed Meowth. "Go and save Jessie and James."

Mimikyu did not respond.

"You said you were going to help us!" cried Meowth angrily. "Forget about Pikachu, you have to rescue my friends!"

With that, Meowth seized Mimikyu and ran after Bewear, Wobuffet following.

Ash and his friends watched them go.

"We didn't get to capture Mimikyu," said Kiawe sadly.

"But there are many other Pokémon in the Alola region," said Lillie.

"That's right," said Ash, "and my Alolan journey has only just started. Let's go and catch some Pokémon!"

The End

DON'T MISS THESE OTHER OFFICIAL POKÉMON BOOKS